May I Please Have a Cookie?

by **Jennifer E. Morris**

Scholastic Reader — Level 1

SCHOLASTIC INC.

New York Toronto London Auckland Sydney
Mexico City New Delhi Hong Kong Buenos Aires

Mommy was baking cookies.

Dear Parents,

Welcome to the Scholastic Reader series. We have taken over 80 years of experience with teachers, parents, and children and put it into a program that is designed to match your child's interests and skills.

Level 1—Short sentences and stories made up of words kids can sound out using their phonics skills and words that are important to remember.

Level 2—Longer sentences and stories with words kids need to know and new "big" words that they will want to know.

Level 3—From sentences to paragraphs to longer stories, these books have large "chunks" of texts and are made up of a rich vocabulary.

Level 4—First chapter books with more words and fewer pictures.

It is important that children learn to read well enough to succeed in school and beyond. Here are ideas for reading this book with your child:

- Look at the book together. Encourage your child to read the title and make a prediction about the story.
- Read the book together. Encourage your child to sound out words when appropriate. When your child struggles, you can help by providing the word.
- Encourage your child to retell the story. This is a great way to check for comprehension.
- Have your child take the fluency test on the last page to check progress.

Scholastic Readers are designed to support your child's efforts to learn how to read at every age and every stage. Enjoy helping your child learn to read and love to read.

    —Francie Alexander
      Chief Education Officer
      Scholastic Education

To Robin and Leo
— J.M.

ISBN 0-439-73819-9

Library of Congress Cataloging-in-Publication Data
Morris, J. E. (Jennifer E.)
  May I please have a cookie? / by J.E. Morris.
     p. cm.
  "Cartwheel books."
  Summary: Alfie, a young alligator, learns the best way to ask for a cookie from his mother.
  ISBN 0-439-73819-9
  [1. Etiquette–Fiction. 2. Alligators–Fiction. 3. Cookies–Fiction.] I. Title.

PZ7.M82824Ma 2005
[E]--dc22   2004031113

10   9   8   7   6   06   07   08   09
Printed in the U.S.A. 23 • First printing, October 2005

Alfie loved cookies.

He loved to smell cookies.

He loved to look at cookies.

But most of all, Alfie loved to
eat cookies.

"Don't grab, Alfie," said Mommy.
"Can you think of a better way
to get a cookie?"

Alfie thought

and thought

and thought.

Then Alfie got
an idea.

He found a big coat
and a big hat.

"I want a cookie,"
said Alfie in a big,
deep voice.

Oops.

"No, Alfie," said Mommy. "Think of a better way to get a cookie."

Alfie had another idea.

He went outside.

Mommy put icing on the cookies.

Then she saw something.

"Get down, Alfie!"
cried Mommy.

"Think of a better way
to get a cookie."

Alfie thought of another idea.
He went to his room and got
some paper.

He cut and he colored.

Soon Alfie had his own cookies.

But he still wanted
a real cookie.

He began to cry.

Mommy hugged Alfie.
"Your cookies look yummy.
May I please have one?"

Then Alfie had the best idea of all.

"Mommy, may I please have a cookie?" he said.

"Yes, you may, Alfie," said Mommy.

"Thank you," said Alfie.

"You're welcome," said Mommy.

Fluency Fun

The words in each list below end in the same sounds.
Read the words in a list.
Read them again.
Read them faster.
Try to read all 12 words in one minute.

he	day	big
me	may	dig
we	way	pig
she	play	wig

Look for these words in the story.

have   **look**   **said**

please   **want**

Note to Parents:

According to *A Dictionary of Reading and Related Terms*, fluency is "the ability to read smoothly, easily, and readily with freedom from word-recognition problems." Fluency is necessary for good comprehension and enjoyable reading. The activities on this page include a speed drill and a sight-recognition drill. Speed drills build fluency because they help students rapidly recognize common syllables and spelling patterns in words, and they're fun! Sight-recognition drills help students smoothly and accurately recognize words. Practice these activities with your child to help him or her become a fluent reader.

—**Wiley Blevins,**
Reading Specialist